characters created by lauren child

I can't STOP

hiccuping!

PUFFIN

Charlie and Lola ™

Text based on
the script written by
David Ingham

Illustrations from
the TV animation

produced by
Tiger Aspect

PUFFIN BOOKS
Published by the Penguin Group: London, New York, Australia,
Canada, India, Ireland, New Zealand and South Africa
Penguin Books Ltd, Registered Offices: 80 Strand, London WC2R 0RL, England

puffinbooks.com

This edition published in Great Britain in Puffin Books 2010
1 3 5 7 9 8 6 4 2
Text and illustrations copyright © Lauren Child / Tiger Aspect Productions Limited, 2010
The Charlie and Lola Logo is a trademark of Lauren Child
All rights reserved. The moral right of the author/illustrator has been asserted
Manufactured in China
ISBN: 978-0-141-33499-8
This edition produced for The Book People Ltd,
Hall Wood Avenue, Haydock, St Helens, WA11 9UL

I have this little sister Lola.
She is small and very funny.
Lola is practising the words to her song.
She is **singing** it with Lotta tonight
at the school **concert**.

Lola and Lotta **sing**,

"*The spring is here,
the cold has fled.
The flowers bloom
and raise their heads.*

*Spring is here!
Spring is here!
Spring is here at last!*"

Then Lola and Lotta
giggle…
and giggle…
until – *HIC!* –
Lola **hiccups**!

In art class,
Lola paints a bird
         with a big tail
and a teeny, tiny beak.

HIC!

When Lola hiccups,
her brush flies
         across the painting.

Arnold says,
"Now it looks like
         an aeroplane."

Lola says,
      "But I didn't want to –
HIC! – paint an aeroplane."

At breaktime, Lola says,
"My hiccups won't – *HIC!* –
go away!"

So I say, "I have an idea.
Look at my finger
very, very closely."

Then Marv jumps
out of nowhere.
"BOO!"

Lola screams.
"Why did you do that?"

Marv says,
"To scare away your hiccups."

And Lola says,
"They're completely gone!"

In class, Lola says,
"The concert's going to be
all right now that
my hiccups have
gone away."

Lotta says, "Oh yes.
Do you like my tower?"

Lola leans in
for a closer look.
HIC!

Lola knocks
Lotta's tower over.

Lola says,
"Sorry – *HIC!* – Lotta!"

At lunch, everyone tells Lola different ways to get rid of her **hiccups**.

She **pats** her head and **rubs** her tummy.

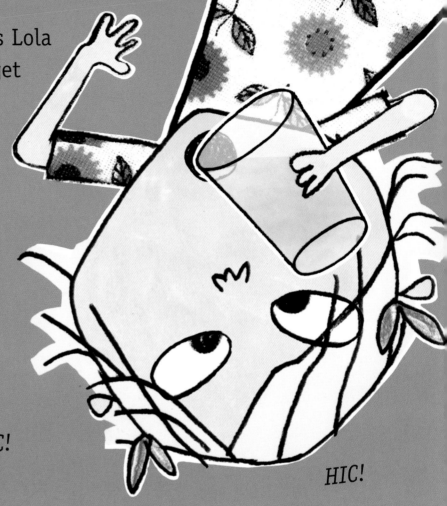

HIC!

HIC!

She drinks from the **wrong** side of her cup.

She says, "AAHHH!"
for as long as she can.

HIC!

Then Lola tries lying
on her back and wiggling
her legs in the air.

Lotta asks,
"Is it working?"

And Lola says,
"Yes! They're gone!"

But later,
during our snack...
HIC!
Lola's **hiccups** come back.

"Ohhh..."
Lola says.
"At first, they were funny.
But I don't want
to have them
ANY MORE."

I say,
"Sometimes things
    can be fun at first,
but then you can get
        a bit fed up.
    Like strawberries.
The first one's always
        super delicious."

And Lola says,
        "But if you
eat too many of them,
        they are not fun.
    Just like my hiccups."

So I say,
    "What hiccups?"

And Lola says,
"They're gone again!"

Lola and Lotta
are backstage
before the school concert.

Lola says,
"I haven't hiccuped
for nearly
one whole hour."

Lotta says,
"Should we have
one last little practice?"

Lola and Lotta sing
their song, and they
giggle and giggle.
Then, *HIC!*

Lola says,
"Oh no! *HIC!*
We'd better get Charlie."

Lola says,
"Lotta made me – *HIC!* –
laugh, and I got
the hiccups again.
How can I – *HIC!* – sing
with the hiccups?"

So I say,
"Try making ME laugh
so I can catch your hiccups.
Then you won't
have them!"

Lola wiggles and
makes silly faces.
Lotta blows a raspberry.

I say,
"Hee hee hee... *HIC!*"

"HIC!"

Onstage, Lotta and Lola
   sing their song.

"*The spring is here,*
      the cold has fled.
The flowers bloom
      and raise their heads.

Spring is here!
      Spring is here!
Spring is here at last!"

Lola **sings** the song
without even
      one little **hiccup**!
Everyone claps,
especially me and Marv.

Marv asks, "How did you do it?"
I say, "I pretended Lola had given her **hiccups** to me."
We laugh, and all of a sudden I... *HIC!*
Marv says, "Very funny, Charlie."
I say, "*HIC!* Now I really have the **hiccups**!"